ELLEN: BOOK FOUR
A TIME FOR
COURAGE
DOROTHY JOAN HARRIS

**Look for the other Ellen stories
in Our Canadian Girl**

Book One: Hobo Jungle

Book Two: The Wishing Time

Book Three: The Waiting Time

Ellen: Book Four
A TIME FOR COURAGE

DOROTHY JOAN HARRIS

PENGUIN
CANADA

PENGUIN CANADA

Published by the Penguin Group

Penguin Group (Canada), 90 Eglinton Avenue East, Suite 700, Toronto, Ontario, Canada M4P 2Y3
(a division of Pearson Canada Inc.)

Penguin Group (USA) Inc., 375 Hudson Street, New York, New York 10014, U.S.A.
Penguin Books Ltd, 80 Strand, London WC2R 0RL, England
Penguin Ireland, 25 St Stephen's Green, Dublin 2, Ireland (a division of Penguin Books Ltd)
Penguin Group (Australia), 250 Camberwell Road, Camberwell, Victoria 3124, Australia
(a division of Pearson Australia Group Pty Ltd)
Penguin Books India Pvt Ltd, 11 Community Centre, Panchsheel Park, New Delhi – 110 017, India
Penguin Group (NZ), cnr Airborne and Rosedale Roads, Albany, Auckland 1310, New Zealand
(a division of Pearson New Zealand Ltd)
Penguin Books (South Africa) (Pty) Ltd, 24 Sturdee Avenue, Rosebank, Johannesburg 2196,
South Africa

Penguin Books Ltd, Registered Offices: 80 Strand, London WC2R 0RL, England

First published 2006

1 2 3 4 5 6 7 8 9 10 (WEB)

LIBRARY AND ARCHIVES CANADA CATALOGUING IN PUBLICATION

Harris, Dorothy Joan, 1931–
A time for courage / Dorothy Joan Harris.

(Our Canadian girl)
"Ellen: book four".
ISBN-13: 978-0-14-305448-1
ISBN-10: 0-14-305448-1

1. World War, 1939-1945—British Columbia—Vancouver—Juvenile fiction.
2. Japanese Canadians—British Columbia—Vancouver—Juvenile fiction. I. Title. II. Series.

PS8565.A6483T55   2006   jC813'.54   C2006-900913-9

Visit the Penguin Group (Canada) website at **www.penguin.ca**

Special and corporate bulk purchase rates available; please see
www.penguin.ca/corporatesales or call 1-800-399-6858, ext. 477 or 474

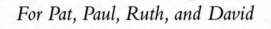

For Pat, Paul, Ruth, and David

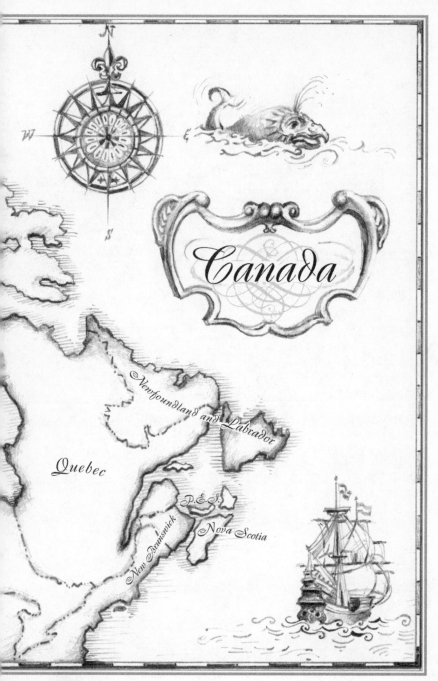

Canada

Quebec

Newfoundland and Labrador

P.E.I.

New Brunswick

Nova Scotia

 Marks the location of the story

ELLEN'S STORY CONCLUDES

W HEN WE LAST SAW ELLEN, she'd been wishing on her birthday cake for the war to end soon. But that wish has not come true. It's now the end of 1941, a whole year later, and the war is still going on. It's not going well either, for England and her Allies— including Canada. England is the only country left in Europe that is not under occupation by the German army, and its cities are being bombed heavily.

But Canada is far from Europe and still safe. Food is rationed, as is gas, but it is not severe. The government is asking everyone to buy war bonds (to help pay for the costs of the war) and to save paper, rags, fat, rubber, and metal and turn them in to special depots. These are all reused and recycled in the manufacture of trucks and tanks and planes. But, actually, the war has not had much effect on Ellen or her best friend, Amy.

Today, with telephones and cell phones and email, we take it for granted that we can keep in touch with people almost anywhere in the world. But in Ellen's day only cities and towns had telephone lines, not rural areas. An urgent message to someone in these areas could be sent only by telegraph to the nearest town and then delivered by car. And since ships at sea could communicate with each other or with their shore base only by means of the telegraph, the telegraph operator was vital to the ship. Knowing Morse code and being able to run a telegraph key were important skills to have.

With so many men in the armed forces, there was a shortage of workers in Canada, and women began to take over the factory jobs. They did the jobs well, too, even the ones that required strength. "Rosie the Riveter" (a worker who could catch red-hot rivets and install them) became a symbol of these new female workers. Women joined the armed forces too, not just as nurses and office workers but also as a host of other things, like ambulance drivers and telegraph operators, as Ellen finds out. Today, when women are doctors and scientists and politicians—to say nothing of astronauts and race-car drivers—it's hard to remember how few opportunities were open to women in Ellen's day. As

Miss Hillman, her teacher, tells her, greater opportunity for women to show what they could do was one of the few good things that came out of the war.

Of course, the war brought many sad events too, even in Vancouver. In an earlier book, Ellen had been afraid that her father might join the army and leave them, which—thankfully—didn't happen. She also worried about her friend Will, who had joined the navy and was at sea.

But as you will read in this book, the war does end up affecting Ellen in a very unexpected way.

*"Do you think that by wishing for some-*thing—wishing really hard—you can make it happen?" Ellen asked.

Ellen Sanders and her friend Amy Takashima were sitting on Amy's back steps. Though it was the end of November, the weather was still mild, and sitting together in the sun was a pleasant way to spend a Sunday afternoon.

"Do I think that you can make it happen?" Amy repeated, a bit puzzled. "How do you mean?"

"Well …," said Ellen, trying to explain, "you know how often I used to wish for a room of my own again, like I had when Mom and Dad and I lived on our own—before we had to move in with Grandpa Sanders. Every night I used to wish that I didn't have to sleep on the chesterfield. I've told you about that lots of times."

"Oh ... yes." Amy looked at Ellen with an understanding smile. "You told me about that. So what you mean is you're afraid that all your wishing made your grandfather die? Just so that you could have his room?"

"I never wished for him to die," Ellen said quickly. "I never wished that."

"I know you didn't," Amy said, nodding her head vigorously.

"What I was wishing for wasn't that he would die. I was just wishing that we'd move back into a house of our own, that's all," Ellen explained. "And once Dad got a good job again we could have afforded to rent a house. Only ... there just aren't any houses to rent in Vancouver now. Not with all the war workers and sailors' families crowding into the city."

"Oh, Ellen, I'm sure your wishing didn't have anything to do with your grandfather dying." Amy's voice was sympathetic. "After all, he was old—and he'd been having heart trouble all year."

"Yes …," Ellen agreed slowly. She did want to believe her friend.

"It would have happened no matter what you were wishing for," Amy said firmly. "I'm sure of it."

Ellen smiled her thanks at Amy, and the two girls sat in silence for a few minutes. A bird zoomed past them. Then Ellen noticed something different in the yard.

"Amy," she said, "where's your swing gone?"

Amy's glance followed Ellen's to the big tree in the Takashimas' yard. The tree had had an old tire hanging from it on a sturdy rope, and the two girls had spent many an hour swinging on it. Now only the rope was hanging there.

"It's gone to help the war effort," said Amy. "The government says they need old tires, and my father says we have to do everything we can to help win the war. He even persuaded my mother to turn in some of her metal cooking pots, because they need old metal too. And he makes sure that my mother saves every little drop of fat and any rags and bits of foil."

Ellen nodded. "Yes, my mother does that too. But I sometimes wonder what the government *does* with all the stuff we turn in at the depots."

"Me too," Amy admitted. "I don't know what it's all used for. But the poster in the grocery store says that every little bit helps."

It was more than two years now since the war had begun. Ellen could scarcely remember back to a time before the war. It seemed to her that there'd always been food rationing and men in uniform downtown, and that her parents had always spent the supper hour listening, with worried faces, to the six o'clock news on the radio.

Ellen sighed. "It feels as if the war has gone on forever. Everyone talks about it all the time. And even the songs we're singing for the Christmas concert are patriotic songs," she said.

"Not all of them," Amy replied. "We're singing some Christmas carols too—like 'Good King Wenceslas.'"

"Oh yes—that's the one where you have a solo bit," Ellen said. She gave her friend an admiring glance. "I wish I had a good voice like yours. I wish I could play the piano too."

"You might not wish that if you had to practise an hour a day," said Amy.

"An hour a day? Every day? Even on a Sunday, like today?"

Amy nodded. "Every day. So I'd better go in and get it done before supper," she added, getting to her feet.

Amy went into her house then, and Ellen slipped through the fence to the house next door. Ellen still thought of it as Grandpa Sanders's house. But it wasn't now—it was theirs. She went up the back steps and into the kitchen, where her mother was standing at the stove.

"Mmm, smells good," said Ellen. "What are we having for supper?"

"We're having stew again," said her mother. "It's the best way to stretch our meat ration."

"I don't mind having stew again," Ellen assured her.

Ellen went to the calendar that hung on the wall and lifted November's page. She wanted to look at December, where the date of the school Christmas concert had been circled.

"I might as well rip this page off now," she said. "It's December tomorrow."

"No, no!" her mother said quickly. "Don't do that!"

Ellen glanced over at her mother in surprise. Her mother's voice had been sharp. "Why not?" Ellen asked.

"It's … it's bad luck," her mother explained. "You should never take a page off a calendar before the next month begins."

"Really?" said Ellen.

Her mother gave her an apologetic smile. "Well … that's what my father always said. He had a lot of superstitions like that."

"He certainly did," Ellen's father put in, coming into the kitchen just then. "Why, I remember how he'd never let me come into your house by the front door and then leave by the back door. You have to use the same door to come in and to go out, he said."

"Really?" Ellen said again. "It's bad luck if you don't do that?"

"*He* thought it was," said her father. He smiled at the memory. "And then there was the superstition about never passing anyone on the stairs—remember that one?"

Ellen's mother was smiling too. "And there was *rabbits*—remember?"

"Oh yes," her father answered, laughing. "On the first day of the month you had to say 'white rabbits' just as soon as you woke up. That was for *good* luck."

"White rabbits?" said Ellen. "Why would saying 'white rabbits' bring you good luck?"

"I don't know why," her mother admitted. "I just know that when I was a girl, we always did it."

"Do you still do it?" Ellen asked her.

Her mother's smile was a little sheepish now. "Yes … if I remember."

The next morning Ellen told Amy about saying *white rabbits* first thing in the morning of a new month, to bring good luck.

"And did you say it this morning?" Amy asked.

"Well … not quite first thing," Ellen admitted. "I didn't remember in time to say it first thing. But I did say it."

The two girls were walking to school together, as they did every day. Last year they had picked up another girl, Marjorie, on the way. But Marjorie had moved away, so now it was just the two best friends together.

"I have a quarter for my war bond today," Amy said.

"Have you?" said Ellen.

"Yes. I have just two more stamps to buy and my book will be full."

These war bonds were for schoolchildren to buy. A quarter bought one stamp, and sixteen stamps, or four dollars' worth, filled a small booklet. Then, after the war, the government would pay back five dollars for every book.

"I still have only three stamps in my book," Ellen sighed. "It'll take me forever to fill mine."

"Well, I earned some money this summer picking strawberries on my uncle's farm," Amy explained. "And then I'm sure to get some money from him at New Year's."

"Lucky you," said Ellen. "You get presents for Christmas and for New Year's too. It must be nice to be Japanese."

"Japanese *Canadian*," Amy corrected her. "My parents are both Canadian citizens now, and they're proud of that. And I was born here in Vancouver, so I'm more Canadian than Japanese."

"Oh—OK, Japanese Canadian," said Ellen. "But it still must be nice to get two sets of presents."

"Yes, it is," Amy agreed. "And I'll have enough to finish my war bond then."

As soon as they reached their classroom, Amy gave her quarter to their teacher and got a stamp to paste in her book. Miss Hillman was their teacher for a second year now, because some of the male teachers at the school had joined the army. Ellen was glad to have Miss Hillman for another year—she was Ellen's favourite teacher in the whole school.

At the end of the day, there was a practice for those who were in the school choir. Ellen and Amy were both in it this year. Ellen always liked to stand beside Amy in choir practice—her clear voice, right in tune, helped Ellen keep in tune too.

On Ellen's other side stood Gordon, a boy from their class. Ellen rather liked Gordon. He sometimes got in trouble for the things he said, but Ellen thought he was funny.

Today, when choir practice was over and Amy and Ellen started walking home, Gordon joined them.

"Hi," he said casually, as if he walked with them every day.

Ellen was a little surprised, but she managed to hide it. "Hi," she answered.

"Did you hear how flat Richard was singing in that last song?" Gordon went on.

"I didn't notice," said Amy.

"Well, he stands right beside me so I can't help but notice. And he makes me go flat too."

"Poor you," said Ellen. "I stand beside Amy, and she's always in tune."

As they walked they talked some more about the choir and about school and about Christmas coming soon, until they reached the block just before Amy and Ellen's street.

"I turn off here," said Gordon. "See you later, alligator."

"Alligator?" said Ellen. "Why did you call me that?"

"Because you're supposed to answer with 'in a while, crocodile.'"

"Oh," Ellen said, giggling. "OK—in a while, crocodile."

As Ellen and Amy walked on by themselves, Amy said, "I think Gordon likes you."

"Me?" said Ellen. "Why would he like me? I'm nobody special."

"Well," said Amy with a shrug, "I think he likes you all the same."

That week at school all the classes were competing to see which class could bring in the most scrap paper. Amy and Ellen had both brought in all the old newspapers they could find from their houses. But after school the next day, Gordon started to walk with them again, and he had an idea.

"I've got a wagon," he said. "Why don't I get that, and then we could call at all the houses around here and ask for their old newspapers?"

"That's a good idea," said Ellen. "Our class might even win if we collect a lot."

The two girls waited outside Gordon's house while he got his wagon, and then the three of them went knocking at doors. Ellen and Amy felt a little shy about calling at strangers' houses, but Gordon didn't. He just smiled and explained about the competition at school. "We're doing it for the war effort" was a magic phrase, and almost everyone found some old papers for them.

After a little while, though, Amy said she'd have to leave them—she had to go to her music lesson. But Ellen and Gordon decided to go on.

"Amy plays the piano really well," Ellen told Gordon. "When she grows up she could maybe be a concert pianist."

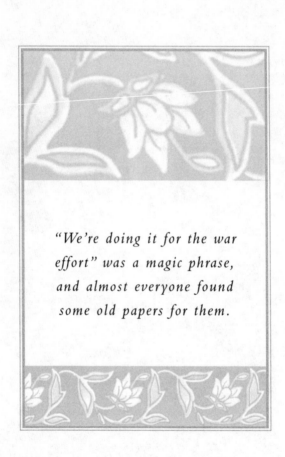

"We're doing it for the war effort" was a magic phrase, and almost everyone found some old papers for them.

"No," said Gordon. "She could be a piano teacher. But women don't get to be concert pianists. Women do things like teaching and nursing and working in offices."

Ellen frowned at that. "Well … not always," she said. "My dad says that women are doing some of the jobs at the factory now. He says they're really good at it too. And there are women in the army— I've seen them downtown in their uniforms."

"Well, yes …," Gordon admitted, "there are women in the army. But they're just doing office stuff, like typing."

Ellen wasn't sure about that—but she didn't say anything more. She didn't want to spoil the good time they were having together.

With all the collecting they did, Ellen was late getting home. Her mother was getting worried about her.

"I was collecting old paper for school," Ellen explained. "Remember? I told you about the competition. And you and Dad are always saying we have to do all we can to help the war effort."

"Yes …," her mother had to agree. "But I'd rather you let me know if you're going to be late. Set the table for me now, please."

Ellen did as she was told. It still felt strange to be setting the table with only three places. But she couldn't say she actually missed Grandpa Sanders. He had always been a grumpy sort of grandfather. And she certainly didn't miss the way he used to go on and on about the war at every mealtime.

The war wasn't going well in Europe—Ellen knew that much from the radio broadcasts. England was the only country that the German army hadn't occupied, and its cities were being heavily bombed. Still, Ellen found it hard to understand why her parents got so upset at every bit of bad news. Europe was so far away—the war wasn't likely to affect them here in Vancouver, was it?

It was easy for Ellen to put all that out of her mind. She had nicer things to think about—like the Christmas concert coming up. And like the fact that Gordon did seem to like her. Ellen couldn't figure out why—she didn't have pretty clothes like Patsy Greenwood did, she didn't have curly blond hair like Gwen's, or even smooth black hair like Amy's.

When she'd finished setting the table, Ellen went into the bathroom and stared at herself in the mirror. She'd worn her hair in braids for years and never thought much about it. But now she tried undoing one of the braids and combing it loose. Her hair looked pretty straggly to her. Perhaps if she washed it, it would look better. But washing it and getting it dry was such a nuisance.

She ended up braiding it again and going back to the kitchen to help her mother with supper.

CHAPTER N⁰ 3

The next morning, as Ellen and Amy walked to school, Gordon was waiting at his street. He had his wagon with him, full of the old newspapers they'd collected.

"I collected lots more after you left," he told Ellen. "I had to tie them in bundles to keep them from spilling out."

"Oh, that's a huge pile!" Ellen exclaimed. "Is the wagon heavy? Can I help you pull it?"

"Sure, you can help," said Gordon. "And Amy can push."

The three of them pulled and pushed the

wagon the rest of the way to school. Then they had to carry the papers down to the basement, where each class had been allotted their own space. It took several trips, but when they'd finished, their class had the biggest pile.

"Look at that!" said Gordon. "We've won for sure."

"No you haven't," said a voice behind them. It was a boy from Grade Eight with a big armful to add to his class's pile. "Ours is just as big now."

"But not for long!" said another voice. This time it was Anthony, staggering in with a huge bundle. Anthony was an English boy in their class—he was a war guest. His family had sent him to live with an aunt in Vancouver to escape the bombing in London.

"Good for you, Anthony," said Ellen. "You've brought the winning pile."

"Well, I have a real good reason to want this war over," Anthony told her, "so that I can go home again."

"Yes, I guess you have the best reason," Ellen agreed.

When they got to their classroom, the principal made an announcement to the school that Miss Hillman's class had won the competition. Everyone in the class cheered.

Then Gordon spoke up. "Do we get a prize, Miss Hillman?" he asked.

Miss Hillman looked at him. "What sort of prize did you have in mind?" she asked.

"Well ... how about no more arithmetic for the rest of the week?" Gordon suggested.

The class cheered again, and Miss Hillman laughed. "No, that's a bit much," she said. "How about no arithmetic today? I'll read you another chapter from *Treasure Island* instead."

Actually, Ellen rather liked arithmetic. But it was fun to have won the competition, and she told her mother all about it when she got home.

"So you see, Mom," she said, "it was worth it, even though I was late getting home."

"Yes, I suppose so," her mother agreed with a smile. "And I brought you something home from my Red Cross meeting today."

Ellen's mother went one afternoon a week to roll bandages for the Red Cross and to pack ditty bags full of warm clothes and other useful things to send to sailors.

"Oh, what is it?" Ellen asked. "Did you bring some more magazines?"

"Not magazines this time. It's an Eaton's catalogue that one of the women was finished with. I thought you'd like looking at it."

"Eaton's catalogue?" said Ellen, taking the fat book her mother handed her. "I've never seen one of these before."

"No, because we live in a city, so we have stores nearby where we can shop. But there are lots of places, like out on the prairies, where there just aren't any stores. So buying from the catalogue is about the only way people have to get things."

"What sort of things?" Ellen asked.

"Oh, almost anything," said her mother. "Take a look."

Ellen sat down at the kitchen table with the heavy book and began to leaf through it. There were pages of clothes to start with—women's clothes and then a section for girls.

"Look, Mom," said Ellen, "there's a pleated skirt here, just like the one you're making for me."

"Is there?" said her mother, coming to see. "How much is it?"

"It says it's $3.98."

"Oh—well, it cost less than that for me to make it," her mother said, with a note of satisfaction.

"All the prices have ninety-eight cents in them—$9.98 or $3.98 or $1.98. Why don't they just say two dollars?"

"Because $1.98 sounds less expensive than two dollars," her mother explained.

"It's only two cents cheaper," Ellen pointed out.

"Yes, I know," said her mother.

Ellen kept on leafing through the book, pausing now and then to look longingly at a pair of pretty strap shoes or a fur-trimmed coat. But as she moved on past all the clothes, she became more and more surprised.

"Look, Mom, there's *everything* in here. Furniture and rugs and curtains and tools and car parts and paint and harnesses for horses ... and toys too and books ..."

Her mother was looking over Ellen's shoulder and nodding. "Yes, I imagine that before Will lost his farm on the prairies, his family did all their shopping from this catalogue."

Will was a man who had come to their door, back before the war, when many men were out of work. He'd done a few jobs for them in return for meals. Now he was in the navy, and he still wrote to them sometimes. Ellen always wrote right back—she thought of that as doing her bit for the war effort.

Now she went on looking through the pages, while her mother started preparing supper. She saw medicines and baking supplies and packages to send to men overseas ...

"And, oh look, Mom!" Ellen stood up and carried the catalogue over to show her mother. "They even have violins for sale! This one is only $10.98. I know pianos cost too much for us to buy, but could we maybe buy a violin some day? A violin would be almost as good as a piano."

Ellen's mother glanced at the page Ellen was holding out.

"But you don't know how to play a violin, Ellen," she said. "You have to have lessons before you can get any music out of a violin."

"Oh," said Ellen, and she sat down at the table again.

After supper Ellen wanted to study this amazing catalogue some more. And now she could take it to her bedroom. But though Grandpa Sanders had been dead for some months, the room didn't really feel like her own yet. Her father had promised to paint it for her when he had time, and Ellen thought that when the walls were painted in the pale pink colour that she'd chosen, the room would feel more like her own. Ellen sat on her bed and pored over the pages in the catalogue that showed bedspreads. *One of these pretty flowered bedspreads … and some of these frilly white curtains … that would make it feel like my room,* she thought.

Still, even as dark and dingy as the room was, it was wonderful to have her own space again.

Ellen picked up her library book and settled down to read for a while. She wanted to finish this book tonight because she'd be going to the library on Saturday. She and Amy always went to the library together on the weekend. And maybe … maybe this Saturday she'd ask Amy to go out of their way a bit and go along Gordon's street. Maybe he'd even come to the library with them—that would be fun. Amy wouldn't mind, she knew. Amy was always willing to do things with her.

Amy is such a wonderful best friend, Ellen thought.

CHAPTER N°. 4

Sunday was another mild sunny day, the kind of day that made it pleasant to walk several blocks to church. Before they left home Ellen glanced at the calendar, which was now turned to December. December seventh … less than two weeks now until the Christmas concert. This was the first year that she and Amy had been old enough to be in the school choir, so they were both looking forward to their first concert. And Ellen would have her new skirt to wear, the pleated skirt she'd been longing for.

At church there were the usual prayers for "all our brave boys fighting in Europe." And one of the hymns spoke of praying for "those in peril on the sea." Ellen always thought of Will whenever she sang that hymn. His ship was stationed somewhere in the Pacific, she knew, so at least he wasn't in danger from submarines, just from bad storms. Ellen sang the hymn loudly and hoped he was safe.

After church, while everyone was standing around in small groups chatting, as they usually did, there was a sudden stir. The church janitor, who had been listening to the radio, was going from group to group with startling news.

"Japanese planes have bombed the American navy base at Pearl Harbor," he was telling them. "They dropped bombs on all the American warships that were anchored in there."

Ellen could see her parents looking at each other in amazement. Ellen was surprised and puzzled, too.

"But—the Japanese aren't in the war, are they?" she asked.

"No, they aren't. Not up until now, anyway," said her father. "Come on, let's hurry home. I want to listen to the radio myself."

Everyone had the same idea, and the crowd in front of the church disappeared quickly. As soon as they reached the house, Ellen's father turned on the radio. Ellen sat by the radio listening as well—she could tell that this was momentous news.

What the janitor had been telling them was quite true. Without any declaration of war, Japanese bombers had made a surprise attack on the American ships based at Pearl Harbor. Many ships had been sunk and many sailors killed. Ellen remembered, with a shock, that she'd been thinking about Will during church and figuring that he wasn't in any danger. But now, maybe he was.

"Where *is* Pearl Harbor?" Ellen whispered.

"In Hawaii," her father answered.

"Would Will's ship have been there?"

"Probably not—just American ones. Now shhh."

They sat without moving, listening to the radio, for quite a while. Ellen was getting really hungry by the time her mother tore herself away long enough to make some lunch. Though they almost never ate in the living room, today they sat there with their plates on their laps, not wanting to miss a word.

To Ellen's surprise her father, though shocked by the news, could see a good side to it.

"This means that America will be in the war now," he said. "The United States has declared war on Japan and on Germany too. So they'll be fighting in Europe as well as in the Pacific."

"Why is that such a good thing?" Ellen asked.

"Because the United States is a big country and a wealthy one. There will be thousands more men available to fight and hundreds more planes and tanks and ships as well."

"Oh," said Ellen. She thought about this for a moment. "But … Amy's mother will be upset— her cousin is a Japanese soldier. He's been fighting in China, but does this mean he might be fighting against the United States now?"

"Well … yes," said her father. "And against Canada too."

"Against Canada?" Ellen gasped. "Against *us*?"

"Well … yes. All the Allies—England, France, Canada, Australia, and New Zealand … and now the United States. We're all Allies together now."

Ellen was silent for a few moments as she ate her lunch.

"Perhaps I should go over and see Amy," she said at last. "She must be upset too."

"No, you'd better not," said her father. "I can see her uncle's truck in their driveway. They probably want to be alone as a family just now."

Ellen and her mother washed up the few lunch dishes, but her father stayed right by the radio. Ellen checked to see if Amy's uncle's truck was still next door, which it was. But she felt she'd listened to enough news broadcasts for one day, and she went off to her bedroom.

On her bed was the dark grey scarf she was knitting. When she finished it, it would be the fourth scarf she'd knit to put in the ditty bags for her mother's Red Cross group. Ellen often tried to make the knitting more interesting by imagining her scarf ending up wrapped around the neck of some sailor far out at sea. Perhaps even Will. But her imagining hadn't ever had that sailor in danger ... with his ship bombed or torpedoed ... with the sailor swimming for his life in a huge ocean ...

No. No, she didn't want to imagine that sort of thing, she decided. Oh, why did there have to be wars?

CHAPTER N° 5

The truck belonging to Amy's uncle was parked in the Takashimas' driveway all that Sunday afternoon. So it wasn't until the next morning that Ellen saw Amy.

Amy came to call for her, as usual, and the two girls set off for school. But today Amy said almost nothing. Finally, Ellen decided to ask, straight out, what she wanted to know.

"Are your parents upset?" she asked. "About ... what was on the news all day yesterday?"

Amy nodded.

"I guess your mother is worried about her

cousin, isn't she—the one who is a Japanese soldier?"

"It's not just that," Amy said, in a low voice. "My mum and dad, and my uncle too—they're afraid."

"Afraid?" said Ellen. "Afraid of what?"

"Afraid that people will blame us for the attack on Pearl Harbor."

"Blame *you*?" Ellen just stared at her friend.

"Yes. All of us Japanese Canadians."

"But—but—" Ellen stammered, "you didn't have anything to do with the attack. You live in Canada—you can't help what Japan has done. It's not *your* fault."

"I know," Amy said sadly. "My parents are both Canadian citizens, and I was born here in Canada. But they're still afraid." Amy looked at Ellen with anxious eyes. "I'm afraid too."

"But … you're Canadian. What can happen to you here in Vancouver?"

Amy just shook her head and didn't answer.

With these fears of Amy's in her mind, Ellen noticed some of the children on the playground staring at Amy and at all the other Japanese Canadians in the school. But once in the class-room, Miss Hillman got them all busy with their spelling lists and arithmetic. She kept them busy all day, and nothing was said about the news. Gordon was away that day, and Ellen and Amy walked home on their own. Amy was still very quiet.

That evening Ellen's father brought home not only his regular newspaper but two others as well. All the papers had huge headlines in big black letters: JAPANESE BOMB PEARL HARBOR.

Ellen didn't usually read the newspapers, except for the comics, but tonight she did. All the papers had the same story: the United States had now declared war on Japan and had joined the Allied Forces in their war on Germany. Canada, along with the other allied countries, had declared war on Japan too.

Ellen seldom interrupted her father while he was reading the newspaper, but tonight she just had to ask him about Amy's fears.

"Dad," she began, "Amy and her family are afraid that people will blame them for what happened. But people won't do that, will they? It's not the Takashimas' fault—they had nothing to do with what Japan did."

"No … it's not the fault of the Takashimas," her father agreed, "or of any of the Japanese Canadians who live here. But people are angry with them all the same. A lot of people at the factory are saying bitter things."

"They are?" said Ellen. Her face showed her worry as she thought about this. "But … Canada is still safe, isn't it? So what could happen to Amy?"

Her father just shook his head. "I don't know," he said.

The next morning Ellen found out what could happen. When she and Amy reached the school playground, Gordon came running over to them.

"Ellen!" he said angrily. "Why are you walking with *her*? You don't want to be friends with a dirty Jap, do you?"

Ellen was too startled to answer right away. "A … a dirty Jap?" she stammered. "You mean *Amy*? She's not Japanese, she's Canadian, just like you."

"She is not!" Gordon shouted.

"She is so!" Ellen shouted back. "She was born right here in Vancouver."

"She's still a Jap," Gordon insisted. "A dirty Jap. They're all dirty Japs."

By now a crowd had gathered around them, and Amy's face was white. Ellen put her arm around Amy's shoulders and glared back at Gordon. "She's no Jap. She's my friend. I thought she was your friend too."

"Well, she isn't, not now. And what's more—"

Gordon's words were interrupted by the bell ringing. Everyone went to line up—and since the girls formed one line and the boys formed another, Gordon had no more chance to talk to them right then. And perhaps Miss Hillman had heard some of the yelling out on the playground, because when recess came, she asked Amy to help her wash the blackboard. That kept Amy safe from any insults for then. But at noon hour, as they began to walk home for lunch, Gordon returned to the attack.

"I'm not walking with *you* any more," he yelled. "Not if you're walking with her!"

"Then don't!" Ellen yelled back. "We don't want you anyway."

Ellen took Amy's hand and they started to walk faster. But it was a very silent walk home. Amy's face was pale and she said little to any of Ellen's remarks. They kept walking quickly all the way home.

Ellen put her arm around Amy's shoulders and glared back at Gordon. "She's no Jap. She's my friend. I thought she was your friend too."

CHAPTER N°6

Miss Hillman kept finding a lot of things for Amy to do during recess. And perhaps she said something to Gordon, for he stopped calling Amy names. But he also stopped walking home with Ellen. She had to admit that she missed his fun—especially as Amy became quieter and quieter.

But Amy's my best friend, Ellen told herself. *And friends stick together.*

Later in the week, though, there was more news. Ellen's father was reading his paper when he suddenly exclaimed out loud, "Oh, no!"

"What's wrong?" Ellen asked.

"There's a new regulation from the government. They've just announced it. It says here 'the government has decided to impose a curfew on all people of Japanese descent.'"

"A curfew?" said Ellen. "What's that? What does it mean?"

"It means that all Japanese people have to be inside their houses before dark, and stay there until morning. They're not allowed to be out anywhere at night."

"But—why?" asked Ellen. "What does the government think they might do in the dark?"

"Well … I guess they're afraid that some of the Japanese who live here might be more loyal to Japan than to Canada. The government thinks they might do something like signal to enemy planes if any planes manage to reach our coast. Or help enemy submarines to land on our beaches."

Ellen stared at her father. "That's silly! The Takashimas wouldn't do anything like that. They *live* here. Why would they help enemy bombers, even if they could?"

"I'm sure they wouldn't," her father agreed. "But lots of people are just feeling very anxious right now."

The book Ellen was reading lay forgotten on her lap as she thought about this. But then a new thought struck her.

"Does this new law mean that Amy can't ever go out when it's dark?" she asked.

"Yes, I guess it does," said her father.

"But—what about the Christmas concert at school? It's next week, and it's after supper. She can still go to that, can't she?"

Her father was shaking his head. "No, she can't."

Ellen was aghast. "But—she has a solo! What about that?"

"Your teacher will have to give the solo to someone else, that's all."

"But—that isn't *fair!*" Ellen protested. "All this war business—it's not Amy's fault!"

"I know it isn't," said her father. "But in wartime lots of things happen that aren't fair."

Ellen went to her room to think. She had never expected the war to affect her own daily life. Food rationing had not made much difference to their meals, knitting scarves and writing cheery letters to Will made her feel virtuous, and the waste paper drive at school had been a lot of fun.

But being at war with Japan had made everything different. Gordon had stopped walking home with her, some of the girls at school were avoiding Amy, and now—now the Christmas concert was going to be spoiled!

Ellen seldom saw Amy after supper during the winter. But tonight she slipped next door and knocked at the Takashimas' door.

Amy answered the door and let her in.

"I just had to come over," Ellen explained. "Have you read about this ... this curfew?"

Amy nodded.

"But what will you do? The Christmas concert is next week! And it's after supper!"

"I know," said Amy.

"And you have a solo!"

"I know," Amy said again.

Ellen was silent a moment, not knowing just how to go on. "What do your parents say about this?" she asked at last.

"They just say '*Shikata ga nai.*'"

"What does that mean?"

"It means 'It can't be helped,'" Amy told her.

"But—aren't they angry? Aren't you angry?"

"No," said Amy. "What good would that do? It really can't be helped."

That didn't seem like enough of a response to Ellen. But the next day, when it was time for choir practice, Amy didn't go. And the music teacher didn't ask where she was. Ellen had to try to keep in tune without Amy's clear voice beside her. And Amy's solo part was given to Gwen, who didn't sing nearly as well as Amy did.

So it really couldn't be helped.

CHAPTER N⁰ 7

Ellen's father often worked late these days.
Since the factory made parts for cars and trucks, it was busier than it had ever been.

"You will get home for supper tonight, won't you?" Ellen said at breakfast. "It's the Christmas concert tonight."

"I'll be home," her father promised.

And he was. They all ate their supper quickly, and Ellen put on her white blouse and the new skirt her mother had made for her.

It felt strange to be going to the school in the dark, with her mother and father beside her—but exciting too. As they walked from one street light to the next, their shadows kept changing. There were other children, with their parents, walking along, and their voices rang as they called back and forth.

When they reached the school grounds, Ellen could see that the whole school was lit up. She had never seen the school quite like that.

Ellen hurried off to the Grade Six classroom where the choir was gathering, while her parents went to find a seat in the hall. Ellen thought she might be nervous being on a stage for the first time, but with everyone else around her, it was easy to sing out strongly.

The next morning, as they walked to school together, Ellen waited for Amy to ask about the concert. But Amy didn't mention it. So Ellen didn't either.

Later that same week, Ellen came in from school to find her mother at the sewing machine working on long pieces of black cloth.

"What's all this for, Mom?" Ellen asked.

"I'm making blackout curtains for our windows," her mother explained. "The government has said that there are to be no lights showing anywhere after dark. So if we want to have any lights on, to read or to do anything else, we have to have blackout curtains at every window."

"Really?" said Ellen, eyes wide with surprise.

Her mother nodded, her mouth full of pins.

"You mean … the government thinks that Japanese planes might fly all the way to Canada? And that we might get bombed?"

"It's possible," said her mother. "Here—hold this piece up for me, will you?"

Ellen held the piece of cloth as her mother had asked, but in her mind she could hardly believe what she'd heard. Bombings and blackouts were what happened in England, not in Canada.

Was it only a few weeks ago that she'd thought the war couldn't possibly touch her here in Vancouver?

The next date that was circled on the kitchen calendar was Christmas Day.

This year, with her father working longer hours and getting more pay, there would be more money to spend, and Ellen was counting the days excitedly.

"Only ten more days to Christmas," Ellen said as she and Amy walked to school.

Amy just nodded.

"We're going to have a Christmas tree this year—Dad promised me we would. Remember how last year your uncle brought you a little pine tree from his farm, and I helped you decorate it?"

*"I'm making blackout curtains for our windows,"
her mother explained.*

"I don't think he'll do that this year," said Amy.

"He won't?" said Ellen. "That's too bad. But you'll still have presents, won't you?"

"I don't know. I haven't asked."

"You haven't *asked*?" said Ellen.

Ellen couldn't understand how her friend could be so uninterested in Christmas this year. But after a few more times when they walked to school, she stopped talking about it. Amy was quieter than ever these days. Then Amy came down with a bad cold and stayed home, and Ellen walked to school on her own. Ellen wouldn't admit it, but she was almost relieved.

The Saturday before Christmas, Ellen went downtown with her mother to choose a present for her father. Ellen seldom went downtown, so she was amazed to see so many men in uniform now—soldiers in khaki, sailors in navy blue, and airmen in air force blue. There were some women in uniform too. Ellen thought they looked very smart in their neat outfits and jaunty caps. Ellen also noticed several Chinese people with yellow badges pinned to their jackets. Ellen managed to get close enough to read one.

"That Chinese woman is wearing a badge that says 'I am Chinese,'" Ellen told her mother. "Why is she doing that?"

"Well ... a lot of people can't tell Chinese and Japanese people apart," her mother explained. "And the Chinese want everyone to know that *they* are not the enemy."

"The enemy?" Ellen repeated. "The Takashimas aren't our enemies."

"No ... we know that," said her mother. "But there have been some unpleasant incidents."

Ellen remembered Gordon's taunts and wondered if Amy's parents had been called names too. Now, as she looked about her, she realized that she couldn't see any Japanese faces at all. Were they all afraid to come out, even during the day?

Ellen and her mother had to wait a long time for a bus to take them home, so that it was dark by the time they reached their street. And that felt very strange—to be outside in the blackout, with no lights anywhere. No street lights and no lights from the houses they passed. Walking to the Christmas concert in the dark had been fun, but this—this was spooky. The familiar houses were great looming shapes, and even the sound of their own footsteps seemed loud. The only person they saw was Mr. Wyatt—he was the blackout warden for their street and he was making sure that no lights showed anywhere.

Ellen was glad to reach their house. They hurried inside and carefully drew all their black-out curtains before turning on any lights.

It wasn't until her mother had supper cooking on the stove that the good smells began to chase away Ellen's feeling of uneasiness.

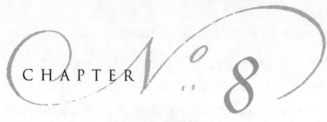

Ellen could still remember, all too clearly, the Christmas when her father had been out of work, and there had been no presents at all. So this year, with a decorated tree in the living room and presents underneath, it was no wonder that Ellen was awake early on Christmas Day.

Her presents were mostly useful ones: a soft new nightie, a sweater, and some mittens that her mother had knit. But there was also a surprise—a little diary with a bright red cover and a clasp to keep it closed and private.

"Since you like reading so much, we thought you'd enjoy writing too," her father told her.

"Oh, I will," said Ellen, opening the clasp and looking inside the diary. All those blank pages … a whole year of her life. *What sort of things will be written on those pages?* she wondered.

Her mother had done lots of baking this year, including a Christmas cake. It was a rich, dark cake with lots of fruit in it.

"There's a superstition that my family had about Christmas cake too," her mother told Ellen as she cut some pieces to arrange on a plate.

"What's that?" Ellen asked.

"My mother used to say that every piece of Christmas cake you eat between Christmas Day and New Year's Day will give you a happy month next year."

"Oh … cut the pieces small then, Mom," said Ellen. "That way I'll be sure to get twelve pieces."

After their own dinner was over, Ellen and her mother wrapped a few pieces of cake to take next door to the Takashimas. They had to turn off the kitchen light before they opened the back door. And when they knocked at the Takashimas' door, their kitchen light was turned off too, until Ellen and her mother were safely inside. Mrs. Takashima and Amy welcomed them politely.

"We brought you some Christmas cake," Ellen's mother said.

"Ah … thank you," Amy's mother said with a bow. "And I give you some of our New Year's cookies."

Ellen had had these cookies before and had not liked them much—but she thanked Mrs. Takashima anyway.

"We … we were all very sorry that Amy had to miss the concert," Ellen's mother said, a bit hesitantly. "Is it difficult for you—not to be able to go out at night?"

Mrs. Takashima just shook her head. *"Shikata ga nai,"* she said quietly. "It can't be helped."

"If we can do anything for you, please let us know," Ellen's mother went on.

Mrs. Takashima bowed her head. "I thank you," she said.

Ellen noticed that her mother didn't mention anything about each piece of Christmas cake bringing a happy month in the year to come. She had the feeling it was going to take more than pieces of Christmas cake to bring any happy months for Amy and her family. There was no warm Christmas feeling in this silent house.

Ellen's new diary was sitting on her dresser, waiting for January to arrive, but Ellen had already written the year, 1942, in big numbers on the first page. And with a room of her own now, Ellen could happily spend the rest of her vacation time reading.

Not that she was allowed to sit and read all day. She was expected to help with all the household chores—like doing the laundry down in the basement and then hanging it all outside on the line. That was a cold, unpleasant job in December, and the clothes were sometimes frozen and stiff by the time they were brought back in. Then there was the cleaning to help with. There was a lot of that to do, especially after the Christmas tree was taken down and there were pine needles scattered everywhere.

It was at the end of the holidays, when Ellen was trying to sweep up the last of the pine needles, that she heard her father gasp. She looked over to where he sat reading the newspaper.

"What is it, Dad?" she asked.

"Oh … this is sad news for the Takashimas," he said.

"What is?" said Ellen, dropping her broom and coming over to his chair.

"Well … there have been rumours for a while that the government might decide to relocate 'all persons of Japanese descent,'" he said.

"Relocate?" Ellen echoed. "What does that mean?"

"It means move them all to a location inland, away from the coast."

"Why would the government do that?" Ellen asked.

"Because they're afraid that some of the Japanese people here might still feel loyal to Japan, and they might help Japanese submarines to land on our coast. After all, a lot of the Japanese here are fishermen and have boats."

"But the Takashimas don't have a boat," Ellen protested. "Why do they have to move away?"

"I know they don't have a boat," said her father. "But it says there won't be any people exempted. Everyone will have to go."

"Well then, what about Amy's uncle's farm?" Ellen went on. "If they have to move inland, they'll have to leave the farm, and that's where Amy's father and uncle both work. What will they live on? And how far inland do they have to go?"

Ellen's father just shook his head at her barrage of questions.

"I don't know, Ellen," he said. "I don't know the answer to any of those questions. And there are more than twenty thousand Japanese Canadians here in British Columbia who will be affected." He gave a heavy sigh. "But I'm afraid it's going to happen. The government has issued what is called an Order-in-Council that they all must be moved inland."

Ellen stared at the newspaper in her father's hand. Her sweeping had been quite forgotten.

"When will they have to go?" she asked, in barely a whisper.

"The newspaper doesn't say."

"And where will they go?" Ellen asked.

"The newspaper doesn't say that either."

Ellen stood where she was, trying to take all this in. She would have liked to rush next door to see Amy. *But what could I say?* she wondered. *What could anyone say about something as awful as this?*

Oh, why did there have to be wars?

9

The next morning was the first day back to school after the holidays. Ellen wondered whether Amy would call for her. She did, knocking on the back door as usual.

Amy didn't *look* as usual, though. Her eyes were red, as if she'd been crying a lot in the night.

Ellen wasn't sure what to say. So instead, she just hugged Amy and whispered, "I'm sorry."

Amy nodded and didn't say anything.

"I know," Ellen said with a sigh. "*Shikata ga nai.* It can't be helped."

"Yes," Amy agreed. "*Shikata ga nai.*"

As they neared the playground, Ellen wondered whether Gordon or any of the others would come over to taunt Amy. And she wondered what she could do to protect Amy if they did. But nobody paid them any attention at all. Most of the girls were clustered together, showing off their new Christmas presents—Patsy had a new coat with a fur collar, Gwen had angora mittens, Lois had a locket with her initials on it. Ellen and Amy stood quietly at the edge of the group until it was time to go in.

After school, too, though Ellen was braced for trouble, no one bothered them. The week passed uneventfully. But on Saturday morning, just as Ellen and her parents were finishing breakfast, Amy came to the back door.

She was crying. Ellen had never seen Amy cry before.

"We have to leave," she sobbed. "We have to leave tomorrow."

"Tomorrow?" Ellen gasped.

"Yes," said Amy. "We got the official order. We

have to be at the train station tomorrow morning. And we can only take what we can carry—just two suitcases each."

"Two suitcases?" Ellen repeated. "Just two suitcases? That's all?"

Amy nodded.

"But … what about your furniture? And your dishes? And your books? Can you take your books?"

"No. No room for any of that. We have to leave everything." Amy choked back another sob. "So I came to ask—will you keep my piano for me?"

Ellen was too stunned to speak. But her father stood up from the table.

"Yes, of course," he said. "We'll keep anything at all for you. Come—we'll go and see your parents now."

By the time they reached Amy's back door, Amy had managed to stop crying and compose her face. Amy's parents were as quiet and polite as they always were.

"We are so sorry," Ellen's father began. "We know you are good Canadian citizens, just as we are. It is so unfair to make you leave like this—"

But Mr. Takashima cut off his words with a wave of his hand.

"Shikata ga nai," he said. "It can't be helped. We must just do as we are ordered."

Amy's uncle was there too, and the three men, with much puffing and straining, set about moving the piano across the driveway and into the living room at Ellen's house. They had to rearrange some furniture to make room for it against the wall.

Amy and Ellen watched all this. But when the piano was finally in place, it was Ellen who burst into tears.

"I've wished for a piano, lots of times," she said, "especially when I heard you playing next door. But I didn't ever want to get one *this* way." She sniffed hard and tried to rub away her tears. Then she turned to Amy. "I'll never wish for anything again! Never ever!"

"Oh, don't say that," Amy told her. "Go on wishing—and wish that we'll be allowed to come back soon—so we can go on being friends."

Ellen sniffed some more and swallowed hard. "All right—I'll do that," Ellen promised. "I'll wish that every night before I go to sleep."

"I've brought my music books over too," said Amy, handing her a pile of books. "You can use them while you keep them for me."

Ellen opened the top book and stared at the strange little marks on the page. "But I can't read music."

"Maybe you'll learn," said Amy. "Maybe you can take some lessons."

Ellen's mother came over to Amy now and handed her an envelope.

"Here's an envelope with a stamp on it and addressed to us," she said. "There's paper inside to write on, too. Will you write to us when you can and tell us where you are?"

"Yes, I will," said Amy.

"Oh … I want to give you something too," Ellen burst out.

She thought hard for a moment and then rushed off to her room. In a minute she was back, with her precious red diary in her hand. "Here," she said, putting it into Amy's hand. "It's a diary. I've written in the first few pages, but it's in pencil so you can rub it out. Will you have room in your suitcase for it?"

Amy looked at the diary. "I'll make room. And I'll think of you every time I write in it."

CHAPTER *N*°. *10*

All day Ellen kept thinking of Amy. Two suitcases ... how could you ever decide what to take? Books were heavy ... but how could you survive without books? And how would Amy survive without a piano? Would there be a piano where they were going? And where were they going?

The next day was Sunday. Usually Ellen enjoyed Sunday breakfast. Her mother always made pancakes as a special treat. But today Ellen ate quickly and stationed herself at the front window, keeping an eye on the Takashimas' house next door. Before long she saw Amy and her parents come out, their suitcases in their hands.

"They're leaving," she called out. "They're leaving now."

Ellen's parents got up from the table too. They all put on their coats and hurried outside. They caught up with the Takashimas on their driveway.

Mr. and Mrs. Takashima bowed to them. "So kind of you to see us before we leave," said Mr. Takashima.

"Of course we wanted to see you," said Ellen's father. "Where are you going now?"

"We go to the train station," said Mr. Takashima. "That is what we were ordered to do."

"Let us help you with your suitcases," Ellen's mother said to Mrs. Takashima.

But Mrs. Takashima shook her head. "*Arigato*, thank you," she said. "But they are not too heavy."

Ellen and her parents walked along with Amy and her parents. No one said anything—what was there to say? A few blocks further along they met some more Japanese Canadians, all with suitcases in their hands.

Mr. Takashima greeted these friends politely. They were all very quiet.

"We will go with our friends now," Mr. Takashima said to Ellen's parents. "We will say *sayonara,* goodbye."

Mr. and Mrs. Takashima put down their suitcases long enough to give a deep bow. But Ellen couldn't leave like that. She gave Amy a long, fierce hug.

"I'm not saying goodbye," she whispered. "Write to me. I won't forget you, I promise."

Amy had her lips too tightly pressed together to speak, but she nodded. Ellen hugged her again and then turned and ran all the way back to her own house.

It's not fair! she kept saying to herself. *It's just not fair.*

Ellen was still saying that the next morning on her way, alone, to school. She felt she would end up throwing her books at anyone who said a mean word about Amy. But no one did.

Inside the classroom, Amy's desk stood empty. Throughout the school, there were many other empty desks. Miss Hillman stood at the front of the room to talk to the class.

"These Japanese Canadians are our friends," she said, "and we're very sorry about what has happened to them."

Ellen kept her eyes on her desk. I won't cry, she told herself. And she didn't during the day. But after school, when Miss Hillman asked her to stay behind for a moment, Ellen couldn't keep back her tears.

"Amy promised she'd write to me," Ellen said, sobbing a bit. "And I promised to write back. Maybe … maybe we could even make a card for her and all sign it."

"Yes, that would be a good idea," Miss Hillman agreed. "And I wondered … are you keeping

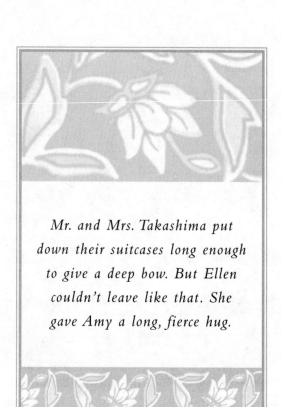

Mr. and Mrs. Takashima put down their suitcases long enough to give a deep bow. But Ellen couldn't leave like that. She gave Amy a long, fierce hug.

anything for her? Because her war bond is here in my desk—it only needed one more stamp, so I bought one to finish the booklet."

"Oh yes, I'll keep it for her," said Ellen. "Or I could send it to her when she writes."

"Good," said Miss Hillman. Then she went on. "I'd keep it for her myself, but I'm going to be leaving too."

"Leaving?" said Ellen.

"Yes. I've joined the army—the Canadian Women's Auxiliary Corps. I hope to be sent to England soon. I'm going to be an ambulance driver."

"An ambulance driver? Really?" Ellen's eyes opened wide. "I didn't know women could do that. Gordon said that women in the army could only be secretaries or telephone operators and things like that."

"Well, Gordon is wrong," Miss Hillman said firmly. "Women are showing that they're able to do all sorts of work now—it's the one good thing to come out of the war. There are women working as ambulance drivers and map-readers and code-breakers and many other things. And there are lots of women doing factory jobs too."

Ellen nodded. "Yes, my dad says they're really good workers."

"And women are learning to be mechanics, and there are women doctors now, not just nurses." She turned to face Ellen squarely. "Women can do all sorts of things—so don't let anybody tell you that you can't. Set your sights high, Ellen."

"Oh, I will," Ellen said. "I promise I will."

She'd been making a lot of promises lately, Ellen realized. But as she walked home she began to think of all the possibilities open to her. *Why, if the war goes on long enough, I could join the army myself!* she thought.

CHAPTER N.° 11

Ellen's mind was still full of new ideas when she opened the back door. At first she didn't notice that someone else was in the kitchen.

Then she saw—and her face lit up. "Will!" she cried. "Oh, it's good to see you. How are you? Are you on leave? Is your ship here? Have you gotten our letters?"

"Whoa!" Will said laughing. "One question at a time. But yes, I'm fine and I am on a few days' leave. And yes, I've gotten your letters. Have you gotten mine?"

"Yes, I even took one of your letters to school to read to the class."

"You did? I hope you didn't show it to your teacher. My spelling's not so good."

"Oh, she didn't care about that. She said it was interesting to hear from someone in the navy. And Will ...," Ellen remembered another question, "have you ever gotten a ditty bag? Mom's Red Cross group fills ditty bags to send to sailors."

"No. I can't say that I have."

"Oh ... too bad," said Ellen. "I was hoping that one of them might have gone to you. I've been knitting warm scarves to put in them. Wait—I'll show you."

Ellen rushed off to her bedroom and brought back the scarf she'd been working on. "I wish it were finished. Then I could give it to you."

"Let's see it," said her mother, taking the scarf from Ellen. "It's almost long enough—I'll just do a few more rows now and finish it off."

"Oh, would you, Mom?"

"Of course," her mother said, starting to knit with nimble fingers. "We'd certainly like you to have it, Will."

"Say, that'd be great," said Will. "It'll bring me good luck, for sure."

"Will it?" said Ellen. "Do you do things for good luck—like saying *white rabbits* on the first day of the month?"

"White rabbits? No, I've never heard tell of that one," said Will, "but a lot of my mates carry good luck charms with them. Oh—hey! I almost forgot." He reached into his pocket and pulled out a folded white cotton hat. "I brought this for you," he said. He unfolded it so that it became a small white hat with a stiff brim standing up all around. "It's a gob hat. I got it from an American sailor—they wear them all the time."

"Oh ... thank you," said Ellen. "I'll take it to school too."

Will seemed pleased at that. Looking at him, Ellen thought how much he had changed from the sad out-of-work man they'd first known.

"You … you aren't so thin any more," she told him.

Will laughed. "No. I was mighty thin—and hungry, too—when you first saw me. But we get good grub in the navy. And I'm learning a lot too—I'm a telegraph operator now."

"Really?" said Ellen. "You mean you send messages in Morse code? How do you send them?"

"There's a metal key that I press—press lightly for a dot and press longer for a dash."

"Oh, I've read about that," said Ellen. "*Dot, dot, dot, dash, dash, dash, dot, dot, dot* spells sos. Is that right?"

"That's right," said Will. "Though I hope I never have to send that message."

"No, I hope you don't either," Ellen agreed.

"But it's a good skill to have learned. As a Sparks, I'll have no trouble getting a job after the war."

"Sparks?" Ellen repeated.

"Yes, that's my nickname onboard ship. Every telegraph operator is called Sparks. And you know what? One of the telegraph operators on shore is a woman."

"Really?" said Ellen. "There are women in the navy too? My teacher has just joined the army. She's going to drive an ambulance. I didn't know women could do all those things."

"Sure they can," said Will. "And they're good at it too."

By the time they had talked some more—and Will had had two more cups of tea and several more cookies—Ellen's mother had finished the scarf and cast off the stitches.

"There!" she said, handing it to Will. "You will think of us sometimes when you wear that, won't you?"

"Sure thing!" said Will, wrapping it around his neck. "And you'll keep writing, won't you?"

"Yes, I promise," said Ellen.

When he had gone, whistling to himself as he walked down the driveway, Ellen went off to her room with the knitting needles, ready to start another scarf.

What a day this has been, she thought. A day of sadness and crying over Amy ... a day of pleasure at seeing Will ... a day of new ideas, new possibilities.

She wondered where Amy was now. Well, she'd promised to write, so she'd start a letter to Amy right now. She had lots to tell her already.

EPILOGUE

Ellen's wish that Amy would come back never came true.

After quite a long time, Ellen did get a letter from her. Amy said they were living at a place called Slocan, in the mountains. They were living in tents and it was very cold. The men in the camp were starting to build huts. They had drawn lots to see which families would get the first ones. They were sleeping on cots, with only one rough army blanket each. There was no school, so the grown-ups had started some classes. Amy was teaching the younger children to read. There was no piano anywhere. Her father had drawn a keyboard for her on a piece of cardboard, and she tried to practise a little on that.

Ellen cried when she read that. She wrote back, and the two girls wrote to each other for three-and-a-half years, until the war was finally over in August 1945.

But even then the Japanese Canadians were not allowed to return to Vancouver and the coast. The Takashimas settled on a farm on the prairies, and Ellen did visit them. But Amy never wanted to come and visit Ellen. The memories were too sad.

Author's Note

Now, many years later, Canadians realize how wrong and unjust it was to intern all persons of Japanese descent, even those who were Canadian citizens and those born in Canada, and to confiscate their property. And we realize how unnecessary it was too, because the Japanese Canadians stayed loyal to Canada.

It took forty-three years after the end of the war for the Canadian government to issue an official statement, a statement of redress, in 1988. The statement had three parts: (1) the government acknowledged how unjust the internment had been, (2) it pledged never to do such a thing again, and (3) it recognized the fortitude of the Japanese Canadians, who all retained their loyalty to Canada.

The government also gave a settlement of money to all Japanese Canadians who were born before 1949. But money can never make up for the losses the Japanese Canadians suffered—the loss of their homes, their boats, their livelihood ... their whole lives, in fact.

Dear Reader,

This has been the fourth and final book about Ellen. We hope you've enjoyed meeting and getting to know her as much as we have enjoyed bringing her—and her wonderful story—to you.

Although Ellen's tale is told, there are still eleven more terrific girls to read about, whose exciting adventures take place in Canada's past—girls just like you. So do keep on reading!

And please—don't forget to keep in touch! We love receiving your incredible letters telling us about your favourite stories and which girls you like best. And thank you for telling us about the stories you would like to read! There are so many remarkable stories in Canadian history. It seems that wherever we live, great stories live too, in our towns and cities, on our rivers and mountains. We hope that Our Canadian Girl *captures the richness of that past.*

Sincerely,
Barbara Berson
Editor

Canada's

1608
Samuel de Champlain establishes the first fortified trading post at Quebec.

1759
The British defeat the French in the Battle of the Plains of Abraham.

1812
The United States declares war against Canada.

1845
The expedition of Sir John Franklin to the Arctic ends when the ship is frozen in the pack ice; the fate of its crew remains a mystery.

1869
Louis Riel leads his Metis followers in the Red River Rebellion.

1871
British Columbia joins Canada.

1755
The British expel the entire French population of Acadia (today's Maritime provinces), sending them into exile.

1776
The 13 Colonies revolt against Britain, and the Loyalists flee to Canada.

1762
Elizabeth

1837
Calling for responsible government, the Patriotes, following Louis-Joseph Papineau, rebel in Lower Canada; William Lyon Mackenzie leads the uprising in Upper Canada.

1867
New Brunswick, Nova Scotia, and the United Province of Canada come together in Confederation to form the Dominion of Canada.

1870
Manitoba joins Canada. The Northwest Territories become an official territory of Canada.